WASHINGTON PARK

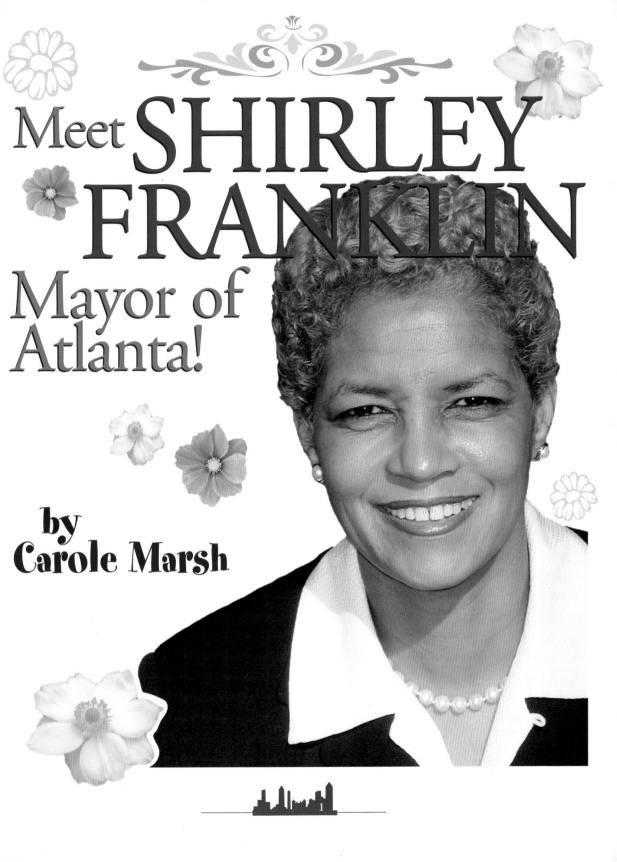

Meet SHIRLEY FRANKLIN

Mayor of Atlanta!

by
Carole Marsh

FIRST EDITION

Published by

GALL**O**PADE™
INTERNATIONAL

800-536-2GET
www.gallopade.com

Gallopade is proud to be a member of these educational organizations and associations:

The National School Supply and Equipment Association
The National Council for the Social Studies

Other Books

Carole Marsh GameBooks™
Georgia Wheel of Fortune
Georgia Millionaire
Georgia Survivor

Georgia Experience™ Products
Georgia Pocket Guide
The BIG Georgia Reproducible Activity Book
The Peachy Georgia Coloring Book
My First Book About Georgia
Georgia "Jography:" A Fun Run Through Our State
The Georgia Experience Sticker Pack
The Georgia Experience Poster/Map

Discover Georgia CD-ROM
Georgia Geography Bingo Game
Georgia History Bingo Game
Georgia Biography Bingo Game
Georgia Jeopardy!: Answers and Questions About Our State

Carole Marsh Mysteries
The Stone Mountain Mystery
The Ghost of GlenCastle

Table Of Contents

A Word From the Author

Dear Reader,

As you sit at your school desk and wonder what you might become when you grow up, you probably have many exciting ideas! Perhaps you've never thought of it, but every successful and famous person was once a child . . . once went to school . . . once made choices and decisions . . . and often encountered obstacles and opportunities—just like you!

As a former school student in Georgia's public school system, I know that this is true! I would sit and wonder if I really *(really, really)* could grow up and become a writer. I wondered if all those history and science and math classes—and all that homework!—would help me achieve my goals. And you know what? They did!

Shirley Franklin probably never sat at her school desk and thought to herself, "Well, I think I'll just grow up and be mayor of Atlanta." However, she knew she wanted to do great things and was willing to study and work hard to achieve her goals. And Shirley Franklin DID grow up to become not only the mayor of Atlanta, but the very first black woman to be the head of a major Southern U.S. city.

Let's meet her!

Carole Marsh
Peachtree City, Georgia
USA

A Story to Set the Scene

Shirley Franklin has on a perfectly adorable bright yellow suit. It is a sunny day in Atlanta, but she is headed to a dark place—the movie theater! Shirley Franklin loves movies! She likes to see one after the other when she can. She cries if the movie is sad. She laughs out loud if a movie is funny. And, of course she eats popcorn! It is rare for the busy, busy, busy Shirley Franklin to have time for a movie or two. But this sunny Saturday, Shirley is taking the time to treat herself. Everything has not always been a treat in Shirley's life. Soon, she will be mayor and perhaps not have so much time for movies . . .

Meet **SHIRLEY FRANKLIN**

Mayor of Atlanta!

A Girl From Philly

Shirley Clarke Franklin was born on May 10, 1945, in Philadelphia, Pennsylvania. She would be an only child.

Her mother, Ruth, was a first grade teacher. Her father, Eugene, was a judge. Her parents divorced when Shirley was nine-years-old. Shirley always gave her family credit for teaching her to be responsible. They taught her that everyone was obligated to help make the world a better place—especially through community and public service. These lessons would take Shirley far!

On My Honor . . .

Shirley was a good student. She studied hard at Dunlap Elementary and Sayre Junior High. Her favorite subject was literature, especially the works of English playwright William Shakespeare! She attended a "girls-only" public school—Philadelphia High School for Girls—and graduated in 1963.

Shirley was a Girl Scout. (Her favorite Girl Scout cookie was chocolate mint!) She enjoyed dancing, especially her Saturday morning classes with her friends. Afterward, her friends and their mothers would go out for Chicken alá King and blueberry pie. Shirley was also

active in the St. Thomas African Episcopal Church. One day, all these varied early experiences would help Shirley in her career.

The Bug Bites

In 1963, Shirley enrolled as a student at Howard University in Washington, D.C. Attending school in the nation's capital was very exciting. Shirley became very interested in politics. She attended the historic march on Washington with her mother, aunts, and cousins. Shirley earned a Bachelor of Arts degree in Sociology.

She Had a Dream

The "sixties" was a significant time in the history of America. It was a time when "hippies" experimented with drugs. Rock and roll and folk music were popular. But more importantly, it was the time when Americans took a hard look at civil rights and began to make changes.

Shirley Franklin wanted to help make changes. She became actively involved in the efforts to achieve civil rights for all Americans. She also got involved in the campaign of another Shirley—Shirley Chisholm. Shirley Chisholm wanted to become president of the United States. Shirley Franklin was determined to help her achieve her goal.

EQUAL   RIGHTS

Even though this candidate lost that election, it was another important experience in Shirley Franklin's life.

Another Teacher in the Family

Shirley continued her studies. She attended graduate school at the University of Pennsylvania where she earned a Master of Arts degree.

After graduate school, Shirley Franklin moved to Talladega, Alabama. She taught political science and sociology at Talladega College.

As a young black woman, it is not surprising that the 1968 assassination of Civil-Rights leader, Dr. Martin Luther King, Jr., had a big impact on Shirley Franklin. This event and other concerns about racism, sexism, war, and other negative aspects of society at that time discouraged Shirley. She responded by becoming more politically active as a voter and a campaign volunteer.

Atlanta's beautiful skyline.

The Move to Atlanta

In 1972, Shirley married David Franklin. They moved to Atlanta. At that time, Atlanta was known as "the city too busy to hate." For awhile,

Shirley was a busy housewife, and mother of three children—Kali, Cabral, and Kai. She was also a busy volunteer.

Shirley worked to help get Andrew Young elected to the U.S. Congress. He was the first African American to be elected from a Southern state since the Reconstruction era. She also worked on the campaign of Atlanta Mayor Maynard Jackson, who became the first African American mayor of Atlanta.

To Serve the Public

Shirley Franklin began her public service career in 1978, when Mayor Jackson appointed her the Commissioner of Cultural Affairs. In 1982, Mayor Andrew Young named her the City of Atlanta's Chief Administrative Officer. She became the first woman in the nation to serve in this role for a major city. This put her in charge of almost 8,000 city workers and a budget of $1 billion!

Suddenly, Shirley was very busy! This was her big break in politics. As you might imagine, many people were watching to see if Shirley Franklin had

Hartsfield Airport

"the right stuff" to get the job done. During this time, Atlanta was growing rapidly. While Shirley was at this job, the city's famous Hartsfield International Airport got its fourth runway and a new city hall was built, as

were a new municipal and court building. Mayor Andrew Young bragged that Shirley "ran the city," while he traveled around the world helping Atlanta become a more international business city.

When Mayor Maynard Jackson was elected to a third term in 1990, he named Shirley the Executive Officer for Operations.

The Olympic Spirit

Hard work pays off! In 1991, Shirley began to work for the Atlanta Committee for the Olympic Games. During the next five years, she worked as a senior policy advisor, managing director for local government and community relations, and as an official with the Equal Economic Opportunity Program. People bragged on her hard work. She did not waste time. She knew how to stay focused, get to the point, and achieve her goals. In 1996, Atlanta hosted the Summer Olympics.

Some of Shirley's "can do" success came from pushing for free concerts in city parks, public art at the airport, better health insurance, an increase in sales tax instead of property tax, and close monitoring of the city's finances. In other words, Shirley gave Atlantans the things they liked, wanted, and felt the city should take care of for them. That included crime-free streets, clean water, plenty of police and fire-fighters, and all the other things that it takes to keep a city and its citizens safe and strong.

The Entrepreneur

In 1997, Shirley Franklin started Shirley Clarke Franklin and Associates, a consulting business. Her job was to help companies which hired her with community relations, public affairs, and planning. She also advised them on how to work with governments.

In 1998, Shirley became a partner in a business called Urban Environmental Solutions. She became active in state politics and was elected treasurer of the state Democratic Party. When Roy Barnes was elected governor of Georgia in 1998, Shirley served on his transition team. In 1999, the governor asked her to serve on the Georgia Regional Transportation Authority and she was elected vice-chair.

Problem Solver!

During her career, Shirley Franklin became known as a problem solver. She did not run away from tough problems. "If I see a fire, I go to the fire," she has said. People admired her ability to see both sides of a situation, to be fair, and to make the right decision.

Shirley was also recognized for her ability to be a diplomat. She could help two different groups who disagreed with one another listen to each other's point of view so that they could better understand each other and come to some agreement everyone could be happy with.

Ready to Rumble!

A political campaign to run for mayor is a full-time job in itself. Shirley Franklin had a big decision to make. Should she run for the office of Atlanta mayor? She knew she could do a good job. But how would it affect her family, she wondered. How would it affect her own life?

Shirley liked to work, but she also liked to garden and have time for her family. In the end, she knew there was only one decision: run for mayor! In 2000, Shirley declared herself a candidate for the elected position of mayor of Atlanta.

In a biography of a "politician," this is usually where you list all the offices that she has run for and won or lost. But Shirley Franklin had never run for political office! Running for Atlanta's mayor was her first attempt to be elected by the people.

In May, 2001, Shirley Franklin "kicked off" her campaign for mayor. Perhaps no other candidate was better prepared for the job. After all, she had run City Hall for more than a decade!

A Handle on Scandal

When anyone runs for political office, they give up a lot of their privacy. Some candidates feel they have nothing to hide. Other people do

not really want anyone prying into their personal affairs. Today, even kids realize that there are many "scandals" in politics. People are often accused of telling lies, cheating, and other things. Sometimes they are guilty; other times, they are not—no matter how much the "other side" tries to convince you they are!

During her campaign for mayor, Shirley Franklin tried to be as open as possible. She posted the names of the people who contributed money to her campaign on her website. She made her personal income tax records public. She said she would not accept fees for public speaking. She tried to avoid any "conflict of interest" between her political and personal activities. You could say that Shirley Franklin has tried to be as "above board" in her political dealings as possible. This helped the public trust her and believe that she would make a good mayor.

In fact, while at her job in City Hall, Shirley did not hesitate to fire employees who did wrong, or punish them with a demotion, or even take legal action against anyone involved in criminal activity. This took character and courage. Remember that doing your job the best you can does not always win you friends or please all the people all the time!

A Race to the Finish!

The mayor's race was nonpartisan and Shirley Franklin had the strong support of many people, especially those who knew her previous work with and for the city of Atlanta. At well over $4 million, Shirley Franklin raised more money than any other female candidate for public office in Georgia's history.

Shirley ran against two other major candidates. She won with just over 50% of the votes. After a recount, she still had enough votes to be elected mayor without a runoff election. Shirley was especially pleased with the support of the women of Atlanta. During her inaugural address she said, "I proudly represent all the women who have worked in the fields, toiled in the kitchen, fought for our rights, and challenged society."

Following a weekend of celebration of her victory, Shirley Franklin was inaugurated into office as Atlanta's 58th mayor on January 7, 2002. She became the city's first woman mayor.

High Expectations

As we learned after the terrorist attack on the World Trade Center in New York City on September 11, 2001, a mayor is very important to a city. Mayor Rudolph (Rudy) Guiliani served an important role in helping the city recover from this sad disaster.

What do Atlantans expect of Shirley Franklin as mayor? They want a

strong leader for the city of Atlanta. Mayor Franklin says, "The people want integrity in their leadership. They want a well-run city that's safe and clean. They want a mayor that cares about them and their city. They want a mayor with experience who is focused and perseveres."

One of Mayor Franklin's first actions was to start a "Pothole Posse" to go out and fill potholes in the city streets that motorists complain about. In one of the first days of the program, 98 potholes were repaired!

At the turn of the century and the start of the new millennium, the city of Atlanta has grown to a population of 433,738. It is a big city with many opportunities and many challenges. A city like that needs someone to hold its hand tightly and help it on its way. Shirley Franklin is sure she is the one who can do this important job!

Off to a Good Start

Here are just a few of the things Shirley Franklin, as mayor, wants to do:
- Create a safer, cleaner city
- Reduce payroll and balance the city's budget
- Return the public trust by weeding out corruption
- Have an open-door policy so that all the people are heard

A NEW FLAVOR!

Just after she was elected mayor, a local eatery created Shirley Franklin Turnover ice cream. The apple pie-flavored treat was named in honor of her refreshing "take charge" attitude, according to the restaurant owner!

On January 7, 2002, Shirley Franklin (pictured in middle) became Atlanta's 58th mayor. Her mother attended the inauguration with her.

Said the mayor, "I want to see Atlanta as a shining example of a livable, lovable, and workable community." She is especially interested in making the city a great place for children and seniors to live. And, she wants to represent Atlanta's very diverse—and still growing!—population.

Georgia Governor Barnes said, "With Shirley Franklin as mayor, the future is bright for the city of Atlanta."

What's Next?

Most kids say they want to grow up and have a good job. What we really mean is that we want to have a good career. A career is a combination of all the jobs and training and work experiences a person has over a lifetime.

Today, Shirley Franklin is the first African American woman to head up a major Southern American city. What might the next stepping stone in her career be? Governor? Congressperson? Senator? Vice-president? President of the United States? Now that you've met Shirley Franklin, keep up with her in the news . . . and we will see!

Things To Know About Shirley Franklin!

- Even though she is attractive, lively, energetic, and always smiling, Shirley considers herself a very private person.

- Although her jobs have often put her in the limelight, Shirley likes to work behind the scenes to get the job done.

- As mayor, Shirley has a staff, but prefers to return her own phone calls and answer letters herself. *"Hello, this is Shirley . . ."*

- In spite of a full-time job as mayor, Shirley also serves on many boards and committees and is a member of many organizations! Just a few of these include: The Democratic National Committee; Atlanta Life Insurance Company; Spelman College; East Lake Community Foundation; and others. In the past, she has served on the boards of United Way, Paideia School, the Atlanta Symphony Orchestra, the Atlanta Convention and Visitor's Bureau, and many others.

- Shirley Franklin has been honored with many awards including: 1995 Legacy Award, Big Brother-Big Sisters of Metro-Atlanta; 2002 YWCA Woman of the Year; awards from the League of Women Voters; Abercrombie Lamp of Learning Award; Honorary Doctor of Laws degree from her alma mater, Howard University.

- Shirley Franklin is accessible. Check out the city of Atlanta's website at www.ci.atlanta.ga.us. You can also visit her at—www.shirleyfranklin.com.

A Day In The Life

8:00 sharp!—In the office ready to go to work, I'm almost always
the first one here! *Return Mom's call!*

Read Atlanta and other newspapers and check any news of
anything that happened in the city overnight. I'm ready to roll!

8:30:   "Meet and greet" breakfast meeting; "I meet and I greet, but I
don't remember ever getting anything to eat!"

9:30:   Telephone interview with a national radio show

10:00:   Cabinet meeting in the mayor's office

11:00:   Attend the General Session of the Georgia
State Legislature at the Capitol

12:30:   Lunch meeting with the Chief of Police

1:00:   Meet with the Atlanta School Board

2:00:   Call Mom to say hello!

Of Shirley Franklin!

2:15:   Have my picture made with Atlanta Public Works workers filling serious potholes in the city's streets!

2:30:   Live television show interview

Call Carole!

3:30:   Meet with my staff

4:15:   Meeting with a Councilmember

4:30:   Meet with Mothers Advocating Juvenile Justice

5:00:   Give award to Atlanta fire-fighters

5:30:   Meet with Carole Marsh, who is writing a biography of my life for kids to read!

6:30:   Dinner meeting   *Plan follow-up meeting!*

8:00:   Home to read reports and prepare for the next busy day!

Shirley Franklin's Favorites (and not so favorites)!

COLOR: Orange

ICE CREAM FLAVOR: Coffee

HERO: Frederick Douglass

"SHE"RO: Harriet Tubman

PET PEEVE: People who gossip

FOOD: Curried chicken

MOVIES: *Singing in the Rain, Fantasia, Lion King*

BOOK: *Temple of My Familiar* by Alice Walker

SONG: "Ain't No Mountain High Enough"

SPORT: Track and field

WAY TO RELAX: Reading (especially biographies of African American women and women of other cultures), gardening (tomatoes, peppers, squash, watermelon, and flowers)

Q&A With the Mayor!

What is one of your favorite childhood memories?

Going to camp in the Pocono Mountains when I was a Brownie! I was a city girl, so I really loved camping out in the woods by a stream.

What advice did your parents give you as a child?

Do unto others the way you would want them to do unto you. Treat people fairly. And, love your neighbor. My mother also emphasized the difference between "getting by" and striving for excellence. She taught me that what you are like on the inside is far more important than superficial beauty or material things. She encouraged me to be adventuresome but cautious, and to have an open mind.

What was one of your first "public service" experiences?

At age nine, some friends and I formed Handy Workers and volunteered at senior citizen homes where we read to the elderly or performed dance routines for them. All through high school, I volunteered as a "candy striper" in hospitals. I especially enjoyed working with children who had incurable diseases and their families.

What obstacle did you have to overcome as a child?

I was very shy. I really had to work at expressing myself and relating to people I had never met before. Perhaps because I was an only child, even as a teenager I was a loner and often depressed about the state of the world. I had to work hard to discover how to overcome these obstacles. Even before I decided to run for mayor, I had to convince myself that I was worthy of leading a city that had had so much great leadership in the past.

Shirley Franklin Says...

A Message to School Students from Mayor Shirley Franklin!

"Your future is defined by the opportunities you take. You must take the opportunities that present themselves to you. Your opportunities are broadened and deepened by your commitment to education.

Education can be training and skills, language skills, literary skills, mathematics, and much more. Using your mind and knowledge is important if you want to succeed in life.

Stay focused and don't get off-track or distracted by external factors or other people. For example, as a young man, Samuel L. Jackson knew he wanted to be an actor. He stayed focused on his craft and his art and became a world-famous actor. Michael Jordan is another example of a person who stayed focused on his goal, and he became a basketball legend. Tennis champions Venus and Serena Williams had natural talent, but they had to develop their talent through hard work and discipline, and they never gave up their dreams.

Take opportunities . . . get an education . . . stay focused . . . and you can be a success in life!"

Questions for Discussion and Other Mayoral Activities!

Discuss the following questions with your family or in your classroom:

What is public service? How do you prepare for a career in public service? What are the rewards of a public-service career? What contributions can a public servant make?

Why do we read biographies of famous people who have achieved important goals or made important contributions? What can we learn from their life stories?

What role does education play in achieving career goals? Does this include early education? How can what we study in school each day help us in our career years later?

Does every famous person have an easy life? Are they just lucky? What role does hard work play in achieving goals? How do we overcome obstacles to achieve our goals?

What does the story of Shirley Franklin teach you about hard work? Overcoming obstacles? Public service? Education? Developing skills? Work experience? Luck? Achieving goals? Reaping rewards?

Things To Think About

Wow! There are soooo many choices.

Mayor Franklin describes herself as determined, compassionate, and thoughtful. *What three words would you use to describe yourself?*

Mayor Franklin says the smartest thing she ever did was listen to her children because "their perspective on life broadens my perspective on life." *What's the smartest thing you've ever done—so far?!*

Mayor Franklin once walked across a highwire 30 feet above the ground, even though she was scared to death! *What's the bravest thing you have ever done?*

Let's see! I think I would like to...

Mayor Franklin says that the events of September 11, 2001 have refocused Americans on the importance of community and unity. "How I behave, present myself, and the qualities I exemplify symbolize the hopes and dreams of the city." *How has "9/11" refocused you and your attitudes and resolve?*

Atlanta Fast Facts List

SYMBOL: Phoenix

FIRST NAME: Terminus

SECOND NAME: Marthasville

NICKNAME: "Big A"

BECAME CAPITAL CITY: 1868; Capitol dome covered with gold mined in Georgia

SIZE: City limits includes 131 square miles

COUNTIES: Clayton, DeKalb, Fulton, Gwinnett, Coweta, Fayette, Henry, Douglas

MOST FAMOUS AUTHOR/BOOK: Margaret Mitchell, *Gone With the Wind*

FIRST MAJOR MALL IN THE SOUTH (Lenox Square)
HOME OF Coca-Cola (the 2nd most recognized word in any language!)
BIRTHPLACE OF Nobel Peace Prize-winner Dr. Martin Luther King, Jr.
HOME OF LARGEST exposed mass of granite in the world (Stone Mountain)
SITE OF the 1996 Summer Olympic Games
HOME TO the Braves, Hawks, Falcons, and Thrashers!
HEADQUARTERS OF the Centers for Disease Control and Prevention (CDC)
HEADQUARTERS OF CNN (Cable News Network)

Further Resources

Around Atlanta with Children: A Guide for Family Activities
by Denise Black and Janet Schwartz

Black Women Leaders of the Civil Rights Movement (African American Experience series)
by Zita Allen

A Heart in Politics: Jeannette Rankin and Patsy T. Mink (Women Who Dared series)
by Sue Davidson and Jeannette Rankin

Epic Lives: One Hundred Black Women Who Made a Difference
by Jessie Carney Smith

Extraordinary Women in Politics (Extraordinary People series) by Charles Gulotta

Kidding Around Atlanta by Roseanne Knorr

Lives of Extraordinary Women: Rulers, Rebels (And What the Neighbors Thought) Kathleen Krull and
Kathryn Hewitt (illus.)

Meet My Grandmother: She's a United States Senator (Grandmothers at Work series)
by Lisa McElroy, et al

Philadelphia With Children: A Guide to the Delaware Valley Including Lancaster and Hershey by
Elizabeth S. Gephart

Political Leaders (Women in Profile series) by Janice Parker

Travels with Max to Atlanta by Nancy Ann Van Wie

Women in Government: Politicians, Lawmakers, Law Enforcers (Remarkable Women, Past and
Present) by Lesley James

Glossary

accessible: someone (or something) that is approachable

achieve: to succeed in doing; to accomplish

administrative: having to do with management or direction

assassination: a murder of a leader or other public figure

campaign: a series of planned actions for getting something done

commissioner: the head of a government commission or department

constituent: any of the voters represented by a particular official

election: the process of choosing among candidates or issues by voting

entrepreneur: a person who risks his or her own money to start a business

inauguration: a formal ceremony for placing someone in office

limelight: the condition of getting much public attention

mayor: the head of the government of a city or town

municipal: having to do with a city or town or its government

obligate: to hold by means of a contract, promise, or sense of duty

persevere: to keep on doing something despite difficulty or obstacles

public servant: a person elected or appointed to a position or job in government

responsible: able to be trusted or depended upon

significant: important; full of meaning

sociology: study of the history, problems, and forms of people in groups

success: the result that was hoped for; satisfactory outcome

Index

About the Author

Carole Marsh is a native of Marietta, Georgia. She grew up in Atlanta, where her father was a Fulton County marshal. Ms. Marsh attended Henry Grady High School. She always knew she wanted to be a writer. In 1972, she started Marsh Media Methods, a public relations and corporate communications firm in Rocky Mount, North Carolina. She won many awards for her work including being named Communicator of the Year. In 1979, she wrote her first children's book, "The Missing Head Mystery," and founded Gallopade Publishing Group to publish and market that book and others. Today, Gallopade International has more than 10,000 titles in print and is located in Peachtree City, Georgia. Marsh is the creator of the Georgia Experience, a series of educational books and materials widely used in Georgia schools; this series recently received a Parents' Choice award for excellence. Just a few of the author's many books include "The Stone Mountain Mystery," "The Ghost of GlenCastle" (based on the former debtor's prison near Grant Park), "My First Pocket Guide to Georgia," and "Our New Georgia Flag."

About the Artist

Cecil Anderson is a native of Mobile, Alabama. He is a professional visual artist with a diverse artistic background, including both graphic and fine art experiences. He attended Platt College in San Francisco, California, where he studied graphic design and production. This versatile artist has created advertisements and other promotional materials. His unique, self-taught style of fine art has been exhibited throughout the Southeast. Anderson designs layouts for many of Gallopade International's appealing kids' books.

Acknowledgements & Credits

I would like to thank Shirley Franklin for all her help with this book. Also, thanks to others who helped check facts, conducted interviews, submitted photos, and provided other input.
Carole Marsh

Editorial Credits

Chad Beard	Gallopade Editorial Supervisor
Imara Canady	Atlanta's Bureau of Cordial Affairs
Susan J. Ross	Mayor's Office of Communications
C. Jade Rutland	Mayor's Office of Communications
Sandra Allen Walker	Mayor's Office of Communications

Photo Credits

Quinn Hood	Cover photo, page 19
N-Focus Photography	Photo of artist
René Victor Bidez, Inc.	Photo of author
Susan J. Ross	Photos on pages 16, 17, 18